P9-DCI-054

WITHDRAWN

903640

donated by

Angelina Remondi

to

North Beverly School

Beverly, Massachusetts

In Honor Of

Mrs. Allen

8965

Grandpa Was a Cowboy

BY *Silky Sullivan* • ILLUSTRATED BY *Bert Dodson*

Orchard Books   New York

Text copyright © 1996 by Silky Sullivan
Illustrations copyright © 1996 by Bert Dodson
All rights reserved. No part of this book may be reproduced or
transmitted in any form or by any means, electronic or mechanical,
including photocopying, recording, or by any information storage or
retrieval system, without permission in writing from the Publisher.
Orchard Books, 95 Madison Avenue, New York, NY 10016

Manufactured in the United States of America. Printed by Barton Press, Inc. Bound by Horowitz/Rae.
Book design by Jean Krulis. The text of this book is set in 14 point Palatino.
The illustrations are watercolor reproduced in full color.

1   3   5   7   9   10   8   6   4   2

Library of Congress Cataloging-in-Publication Data
Sullivan, Silky. Grandpa was a cowboy / by Silky Sullivan ; illustrated by Bert Dodson.   p.   cm.
''A Richard Jackson book''—Half t.p. Summary: A young boy, raised by his aunt and uncle, shares a special visit
with his grandfather and learns about his family's past and the old man's life as a cowboy and raising a family in the
Ozark mountains. ISBN 0-531-09511-8—ISBN 0-531-08861-8 (lib. bdg.).   [1. Grandfathers—Fiction.
2. Orphans—Fiction.   3. Mountain life—Fiction.]   I. Dodson, Bert, ill.   II. Title.
PZ7.S9537Gr   1996   [E]—dc20   95-21454

To the memory of two grandfathers who were cowboys

J. D. W. Sullivan
June 1, 1888–June 20, 1960
　　　　　　　　—S.S.

Wynn Kilgore
　　　—B.D.

Grandpa came on the train, alone.
He was tall and thin, with white hair and
a white shirt. He carried a brown paper
bag.

Auntie said he should have a suitcase. He said a paper bag was fine.

On the way home, Grandpa sat with me in the backseat of Uncle's brand-new car. He let me peek inside the paper bag. It held a clean shirt and a pair of socks rolled into a ball.

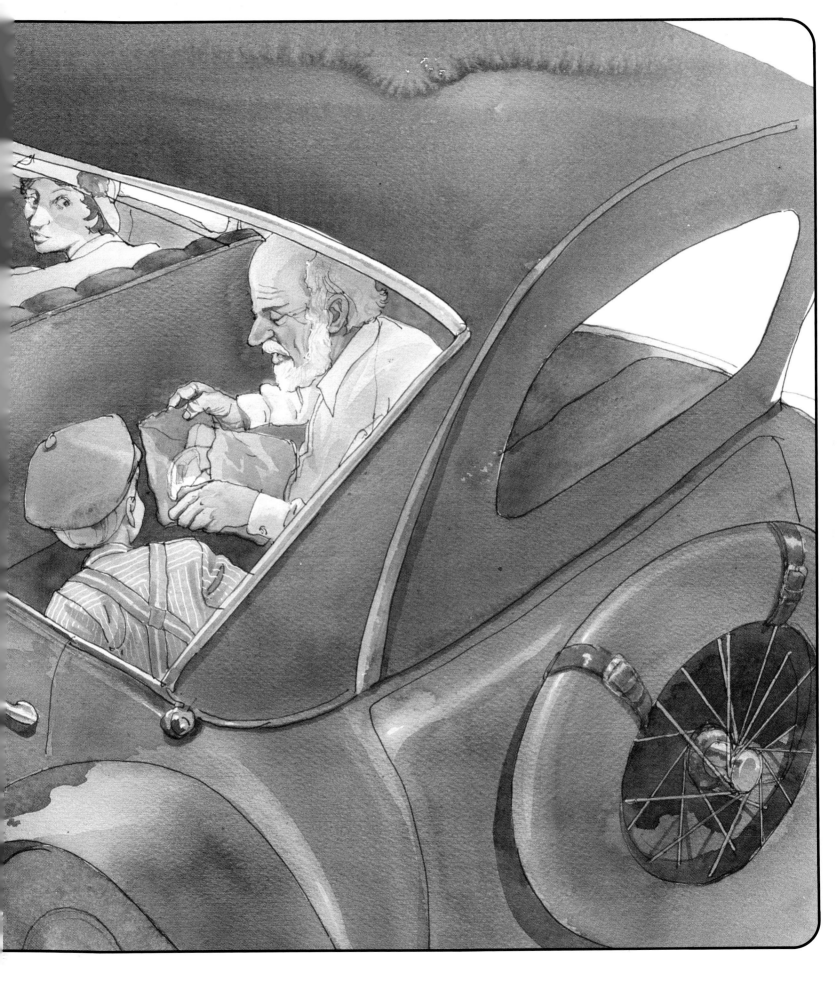

Auntie showed Grandpa all around her new house. "Don't you
love it?" she said. "Isn't it pretty?" she said. Grandpa said it was fine.
Uncle brought in a tin can so Grandpa could spit tobacco juice.
Auntie didn't like that—she sniffed and went out to the kitchen.

Grandpa told me how he used to be a cowboy. When he was thirteen years old, he drove longhorn cattle all the way from Texas through the Oklahoma Indian Territory to Fort Smith, Arkansas, where they were bought by the army. He had a pretty pinto pony. He had a pair of fancy Spanish spurs called rowels.

He had a heavy silver ring, handmade in Mexico, with elkhorn ivory set in it.

He saw Indians many times.

When he was twenty-one, Grandpa rode through the Ozarks
with a camera strapped to his horse's back. The camera stood on
long legs that folded. It had a black cloth to put over your head
when you took pictures. That was how he met my grandma.

Grandma and her family had come west in a covered wagon. Every
morning, they milked the cow, then hung the bucket under the wagon.
By the time they stopped for supper, the jolting of the wagon had churned
the milk to butter. They ate it spread on hot corn bread they had cooked
over an open fire. They slept under the stars. The next morning, they
milked the cow again and hung the bucket under the wagon. . . .

But Grandma and her family did not like the Oklahoma Indian Territory; it was too flat, there were no trees upon it. They settled in the Ozarks instead, where there were woods and streams to hunt and fish in and logs to build a cabin. That was where Grandpa found her.

He took her picture and she took his heart. It was time to settle down.

Grandpa and Grandma built their own little cabin on the side of a mountain. They raised sorghum to make molasses for sweetener. They raised popcorn and peanuts. They raised real corn to feed the hogs and cattle that grazed wild in the woods. (If you didn't feed them corn once a day, they ran away altogether!)

They raised eleven children. Uncle was one. My father was another. "He was my youngest," Grandpa said, "the only one to stay with me on the farm—till he went to be a soldier."

"I have a picture of him," I said. "There's a medal on it."

We looked at the picture. "He was too young to be no soldier," Grandpa said, "but he done good. They told me so." His hand trembled, touching the photograph.

"Wish I had known him," I said. "And my mama."

Grandpa sighed. "Those were hard times," he said. "She got sick after you were born and no one knew what to do about it." He put the photograph back in my hands. "That's when he went to be a soldier," he said. "After she died."

It made me sad to think about my mother. "I don't have a picture of her," I said.

Grandpa put a hand on my shoulder. "That's all right. She knows you love her just the same."

Grandpa slept in my room that night. He thought my blanket with cowboys and Indians on it was mighty fine. His mattress at home was stuffed with corn shucks, he said. When Grandma was alive, she used to stuff the mattress herself with corn shucks she had dried in her own garden.

Grandma made her own soap, too. She boiled lye and wood ash and lard in a big kettle in the backyard. When it had cooked long enough, she poured the soap into wooden troughs to cool. Then she broke it into chunks.

Grandma's soap was so strong, it took the skin right off your back. But her kids were clean!

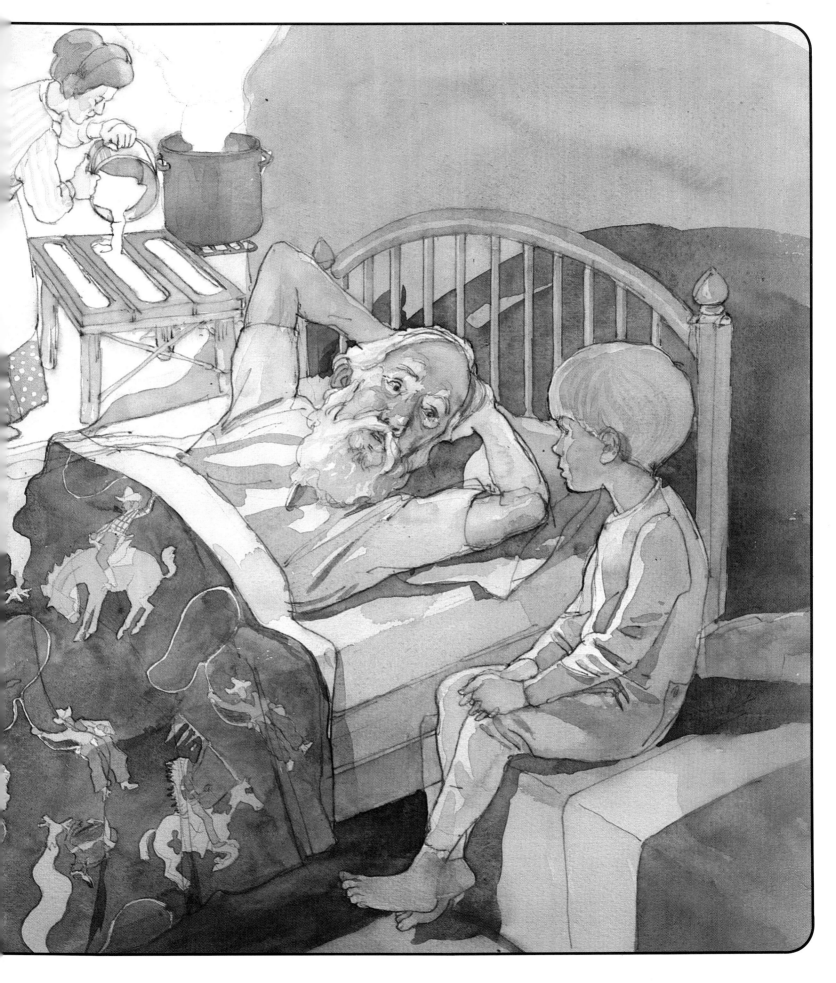

At night, they used to gather around the fireplace in the cabin and sing songs and tell stories. They popped corn and made peanut brittle. Every night was like a party when you had eleven children!

"Grandpa," I said, "I want to go live with you in the mountains. I want to raise popcorn and peanuts, and feed the hogs so they won't run away in the woods."

Grandpa squeezed my hand in the dark. "Only trouble with us," he said, "is you're too young and I'm too old. Can't turn back the clock, can we?" He squeezed my hand again. " 'Sides, ain't Uncle and Auntie good to you?"

"Yes, sir," I said. "But she's awful particular about her house."

Grandpa chuckled. "She got a right to be particular," he said. "Your uncle come out of them mountains and made a good livin' for her." He sighed, looking into the darkness. "Wouldn't we be somethin', though? Just you and me, out there on the side of the mountain."

We fell asleep and dreamed of it.

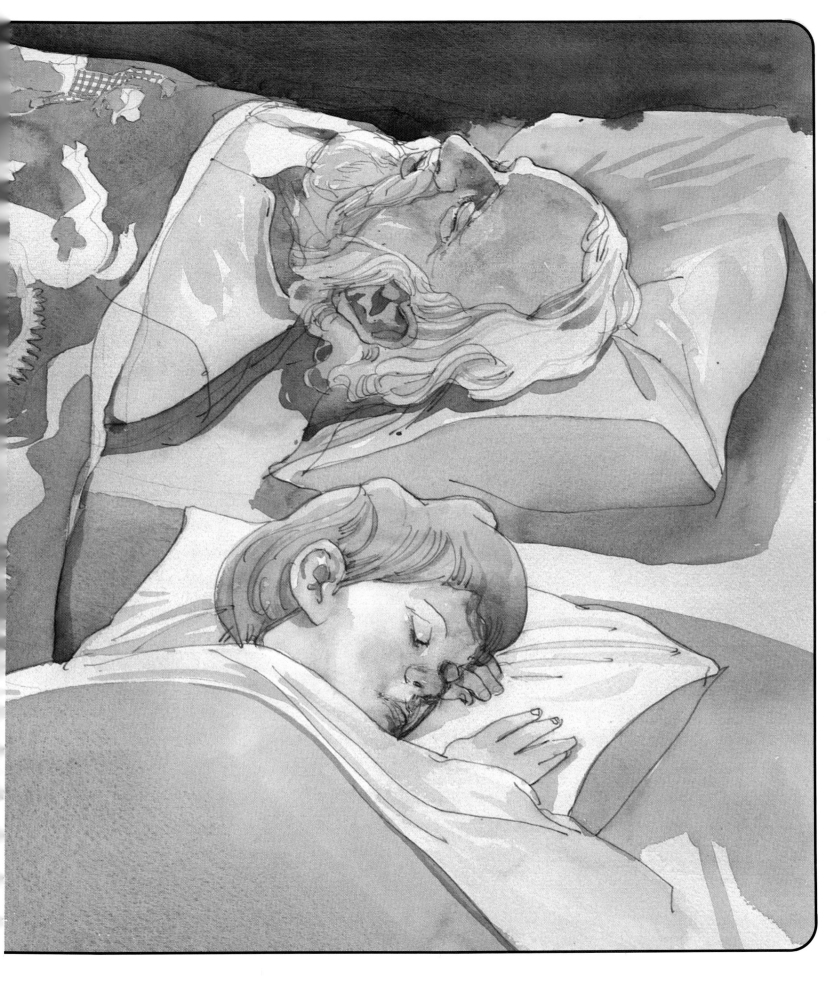

Grandpa didn't stay with us very long. He couldn't make himself go to the bathroom inside a house. It felt dirty, he said. He missed his johnny house behind the log cabin.

Uncle and I drove Grandpa to the station. They shook hands. "I won't be back," Grandpa said. "It's too far and I'm too old." He shook my hand, too. "You be proud, hear?" I looked at what he left in my hand—a heavy silver ring, handmade in Mexico, with elkhorn ivory set in it.

Grandpa went back on the train, alone. He was tall and thin, with white hair and a white shirt. He carried a brown paper bag. I never saw him again.

I never forgot him.